D0443277

IT'S NOT ABOUT THE
DIAMONDS!

WITHDRAWN

Veronika Martenova Charles

Illustrated by David Parkins

TUNDRA BOOKS

Published in Canada by Tundra Books, a division of Random House of Canada Limited,
One Toronto Street, Suite 300, Toronto, Ontario M5C 2V6

Published in the United States by Tundra Books of Northern New York,
P.O. Box 1030, Plattsburgh, New York 12901

Library of Congress Control Number: 2012945431

Library and Archives Canada Cataloguing in Publication

Charles, Veronika Martenova
     It's not about the diamonds! / Veronika Martenova Charles ; illustrated
by David Parkins.

(Easy-to-read wonder tales)
Short stories based on Diamonds and toads tales from around the world.
ISBN 978-1-77049-328-5. – ISBN 978-1-77049-333-9 (EPUB)

     1. Fairy tales. I. Parkins, David II. Title. III. Series: Charles,
Veronika Martenova. Easy-to-read wonder tales.

PS8555.H42242I8333 2013   jC813'.54   C2012-905308-2

We acknowledge the financial support of the Government of Canada through the
Canada Book Fund and that of the Government of Ontario through the Ontario Media
Development Corporation's Ontario Book Initiative. We further acknowledge the support of
the Canada Council for the Arts and the Ontario Arts Council for our publishing program.

ONTARIO ARTS COUNCIL
CONSEIL DES ARTS DE L'ONTARIO

Edited by Stacey Roderick

www.tundrabooks.com

Printed and bound in China

1 2 3 4 5 6   18 17 16 15 14 13

CONTENTS

LUNCHTIME
PART 1

"What are you eating?"

Jake asked Lily at lunchtime.

"Cherries," replied Lily.

"Can we have some?" asked Jake.

"Sure," said Lily. "Cherries,

phlit, are my, *phlit*,

favorite fruit, *phlit*."

Ben looked at the pits

dropping from her mouth.

"That reminds me of a story I know
about a girl who had diamonds
fall out of her mouth," said Ben.
"I know a story like that," said Jake.
"But it's not about diamonds.
I'll tell it to you."

THREE GNOMES

(*Diamonds and Toads* from Germany)

Once there was a girl called Ema

who lived with her stepmother

and stepsister.

The stepmother was cruel

and made life very hard for Ema.

One winter, when the snow was deep,

the stepmother made a dress

out of paper.

She called Ema and said,

"Now put on this dress,

go to the forest, and bring me

a basket of strawberries.

I have a craving for them."

"How can I?" Ema said.

"Strawberries don't grow in winter.

And I will freeze in that dress."

"How dare you talk to me

like that!" shouted her stepmother.

"Go and don't come back
without the basket of strawberries."
Then she gave Ema a piece of bread
and said, "Here is your food."
Ema put on the paper dress
and went out into the snow.

She walked into the forest

and found a small cottage.

Three little gnomes were looking

out of the window.

Ema knocked on the door.

"Come in," called the gnomes.

Glad to be out of the cold,

Ema sat down by the fire

to eat her bread.

"Can we have some, too?"

asked the gnomes.

"Of course," replied Ema

and divided the bread into pieces.

"What are you doing in the forest?"

the gnomes asked.

"I'm looking for strawberries,"

answered Ema.

"I can't go back until

I have a basket full."

After she finished eating,

the gnomes asked her

to sweep the snow away

from the back door.

Once Ema was outside,

the gnomes began talking.

"What should we give her

for being so kind?" asked one.

"Let's make a piece of gold

drop from her mouth

each time she speaks,"

said the other two gnomes.

Meanwhile, Ema swept the snow

away from the back of the house.

What do you think she found?

Strawberries!

Ema filled the basket,

thanked the little gnomes,

and rushed back home.

When she entered the house

and said, "Good evening,"

a piece of gold fell out of her mouth.

Then she explained

what had happened to her

and, with each word,

more gold fell out.

Her stepsister was jealous.

She pleaded with her mother

to let her go

and look for strawberries, too.

Finally, her mother gave in.

The girl put on a fur coat,

took a cake her mother had baked,

and headed straight for the cottage.

The three gnomes were looking

out of the window.

The girl barged in uninvited,

settled by the fire,

and began to stuff herself

with the cake.

"Please, can you give us some?"

the little men asked.

But the girl answered,

"There's hardly enough for me.

Get your own food."

When she finished eating,

the gnomes asked her,

"Can you please sweep the snow

by the back door?"

"Do it yourself!" the girl said.

"I'm not your servant."

Then she went outside

to get the strawberries.

When she didn't find any,

she went home in a bad mood.

Meanwhile, the three gnomes

were talking among themselves.

"What should we give her

for being so greedy and rude?"

asked one.

"Let a toad jump out of her mouth

each time she says a word,"

said the other two gnomes.

When the girl arrived home

and began telling her mother

what happened,

a toad jumped out of her mouth

with every word she spoke.

From then on,

people wouldn't go near her.

She had to live alone

and soon died in misery.

★ ★ ★

"Once when I was eating dinner,"

said Ben, "I sneezed,

and a piece of chicken

flew out of my nose!"

"That's gross!" said Lily.

"Anybody want a rice cake?"

asked Jake.

"Yes, please," said Lily and Ben.

"Hey, I know a story

about rice cakes," said Ben.

"Do they fall out of

somebody's nose?" asked Lily.

"No," said Ben.

"But it's a good story."

★

RICE CAKES

(*Diamonds and Toads* from Indonesia)

Elok and Lia were sisters.

Elok was older and kind,

and Lia was lazy and clever.

Lia always figured out

how to get out of doing

any work in the house.

One day, their mother said,

"I'm going to the market.

Go pick the rice in the field

and make rice cakes for dinner."

After she left, Lia said to Elok,

"I don't feel well. My head hurts.

Can you please go pick the rice?

I'll clean it when you get back."

"All right," said Elok.

"I hope you feel better soon."

Elok worked hard in the hot field,

and when the baskets were filled

she brought them home.

Her sister was sitting under a tree

fanning herself.

"I just remembered," said Lia,

"I have to do something.

Please clean and grind the rice.

I'll be right back."

Then she raced to the river

and went for a swim in cool water.

Meanwhile, Elok cleaned the rice,

ground it into flour,

and made the rice cakes.

She was covered with sweat

from all her hard work.

In the afternoon, Lia came back.

"Go and clean yourself,"

Lia told Elok.

"I will finish the cooking

before Mother returns."

After Elok left,

Lia sprinkled flour and water

on her face so it would look

like she was sweating.

Just then, their mother returned.

"I'm so glad you're here," said Lia.

"I have worked hard all day

while Elok went swimming."

Their mother was angry.

When Elok came back,

she beat her and screamed,

"How dare you let your sister

do all the work?

Now, take these dirty clothes

and wash them in the river."

Elok went off crying.

She washed the clothes

and spread them out to dry.

By then, she was so tired

that she fell asleep.

When she awoke, it was dark.

She stumbled through the jungle,

not knowing which way to go.

Finally, she saw a hut in a clearing.

All kinds of jungle animals

surrounded the little house.

An old woman came out of the door.

"Don't be afraid," she said.

"The animals won't harm you.

Come in and have something to eat."

Elok ate dinner with the woman

and then lay down to sleep.

In the morning,

Elok tidied up

the woman's house

and weeded the garden.

She stayed with the woman

for weeks.

One day, Elok said,

"I must go back home.

I miss my mother and sister."

"Of course," the woman replied,

and she gave Elok a small box.

"This is a gift for all your help.

Don't open it until you get home."

Elok carried the box

through the jungle to her village.

Finally home, she opened it.

Inside were jewels and rings!

She put some on.

Just then, Lia returned from the

field. She looked very tired

because she had to work so hard

while Elok was gone.

She saw the jewels

and became jealous.

Then Elok told her what happened.

"I'll get myself some jewels, too,"

said Lia, and she rushed off.

She wandered through the jungle

until she found the clearing

with the animals and the house.

BANG! BANG!

She pounded on the door.

The old woman opened the door.

"I'm hungry," said Lia.

"Bring me some food!"

Lia ate everything in the pot

the woman put on the table

and then took a nap in the shade.

When she woke up,

she asked the old woman,

"Can you give me a gift

like you gave my sister?"

The woman brought a small box

and told Lia not to open it

before she got home.

But as soon as Lia was back

in the jungle, she stopped

and opened the box.

Out came big spiders

that bit her all over!

"Ahhhhhhh!" Lia screamed

and ran to the village.

"What happened?" asked Elok.

Then she put some healing

leaves on Lia's spider bites

to take the pain away.

"I am so lucky to have you

as my sister!" cried Lia.

"I'll never be jealous again."

From that time, Lia shared

the work equally with Elok,

and they lived happily together.

"Yuck! I hate spiders," said Jake.

"I wonder how big they were."

"It doesn't matter," said Lily.

"Sometimes it's the small bugs

that are deadly,

like the germs in one story

I've heard."

"What's the story?"

asked Ben.

"It's about two brothers ..."

Lily began.

★

OLD MAN OF THE RIVER

(*Diamonds and Toads* from Africa)

Long ago, in a village,

lived a man with two sons,

Tobi and Uba.

Tobi was nice and quiet,

but Uba liked to fight and argue.

One afternoon, their father said,

"Go fetch some water!"

Tobi took a big water jar

and set out on the road

with his brother.

But as soon as their hut

was out of sight,

Uba said, "I'm not going!"

and went to play with friends.

So Tobi went alone.

When he reached the river,

he tried to dip the jar in.

Slish! Tobi slid in the mud

and fell into the water.

The undertow pulled him down

into a large cave

on the side of the riverbank.

There, Tobi saw a pot of food

cooking in the shadow.

A voice came from inside saying,

"Stir me and eat me!"

Tobi was hungry,

so he stirred the food in the pot

and then ate some.

"Thank you so much!" he said.

"These are the best yams

I have ever tasted."

Then Tobi noticed an old man

in the back of the cave.

Beside him were several clay pots.

"Come closer," the old man said.

Tobi walked over to him

and thanked him for the meal.

"My child," the man said.

"I see that you have good manners.

Choose one of these pots as a gift

and take it to the other world."

Tobi didn't want to be greedy,

so he chose a small, plain pot.

Then he thanked the old man

and returned through the water

to the dry land.

When Tobi arrived back home,

he looked inside the pot.

It was filled with golden coins!

He showed his father and brother

his gift and told them

what happened.

Uba was jealous.

"Why should my brother

be so lucky?" he thought.

So he went to the river

and jumped in.

He found the cave

and saw the pot cooking by itself.

Not waiting for an invitation,

he ate all the food inside it.

Next, he looked around

and saw the old man

sitting in the back of the cave.

"You there!" Uba shouted.

"What have you got for me?"

"My child," the old man replied.

"You have no manners.

Still, I'll offer you a gift.

But take my advice

and choose the smallest one."

But Uba did not listen.

"I want the big pot," he said rudely.

"There will be more inside."

Without a word of thanks,

Uba grabbed the largest pot

and swam up to the riverbank.

He stuck his hand inside the pot

to see what was there.

But the one that had looked best

had the worst contents.

Inside were germs of a disease!

They attached to Uba's hand

and quickly spread up his arm.

Soon his body swelled up

to an enormous size.

Uba ran home, but his father and

brother didn't recognize him.

"*A monster!*" they screamed

and then fled in terror,

leaving the greedy boy all alone.

And since they never went back,

Uba may still be there.

★ ★ ★

LUNCHTIME
PART 2

"Wow, that was scary," said Ben.

"And what are yams?" asked Jake.

"They look like potatoes,

but they're sweet," Lily replied.

"I've never had one," said Jake.

"Me, neither," said Ben.

"You know what?" said Lily.

"I'll ask my mom to cook some,

and I'll bring them

for my lunch tomorrow.

You can have a taste!"

"Great!" said Jake.

"I'll bring some strawberries."

"And I'll bring potato chips,"

said Ben. "We can eat those after."

★

ABOUT THE STORIES

Diamonds and Toads might be the best known of the stories belonging to a type of tale called "The Kind and the Unkind Girls." Over a thousand of these tales have been found around the world. Here are three of them:

Three Gnomes is a story from Germany, and this is my retelling of the Grimms' tale *The Three Little Gnomes in the Forest*.

Rice Cakes is based on a story from Bali, Indonesia, called *Red Onion, White Onion*.

Old Man of the River comes from the Kikuyu people in Kenya, Africa, where it's called *Cook, Eat and Carry Me*. In my version, I changed the two sisters to two brothers.